A STORY ABOUT SELLING
A RANCH

WES ST. CLAIR

St. John Publishing Company

ISBN: 978-1-7348970-0-5 (trade paperback)
ISBN: 978-1-7348970-1-2 (ebook)

St. John Publishing Company
1187 Coast Village Road
Suite 1 #249
Santa Barbara, CA 93108

Cover design by Victoria Davies

To All Sellers

CONTENTS

PREFACE

Although I've been a real estate broker in California for the past 20 years, I still consider myself somewhat of an outsider. I worked in the banking business for 35 years before jumping into real estate, and that background helps me to observe transactions from a slightly unconventional viewpoint.

I've always been fascinated with properties that take a long time to sell and cause the owner to settle for a greatly reduced closing price. When a seller and an agent try to sell a property for more than it's worth, one cannot help but ask, "Why did they choose that price?" and "What could they have done differently?" This story is a satiric attempt to answer those questions.

It is important to note that these pages are not an instruction manual on how to sell real estate; competent real estate professionals should always be consulted. Although the ranch in this book is completely fictional, if we are ever lucky enough to own a jewel like The Lazy J, I hope we would have the wisdom to know its value in both an objective and subjective sense.

Wes St. Clair
April 2020

Jack Morrison owned a large ranch in Montana that he wanted to sell.

The property consisted of 70,000 deeded acres and 30,000 leased acres with a 20,000 square-foot ranch house and three additional residences, plus barns, stables, a racetrack, an aircraft hangar, an 18-hole golf course and a 5000-foot runway that could accommodate private jets. Jack had made most of these improvements after he purchased the site twenty years ago and renamed it The Lazy J. J stood for "Jack", of course. The ranch had been a successful working operation when he'd bought it, and for two decades it had fulfilled Jack's desire to own vast stretches of land while giving him the ability to step outside his door and either play a round of golf or fly off to another state.

The thought of selling his property and moving to town held no appeal until recently, when his wife had started spending more time at the local country club than at the ranch. The club had rebuilt their course using a designer Jack had recommended, and the county had improved the local airport, making Jack reconsider the need for his own golf course and private runway. When the airport commissioner called to say that they had reserved space for him to build a hangar to his specifications, Jack felt that the last piece had fallen in place. It was time to scale down and finally sell The Lazy J.

He knew his ranch was worth at least 110 million. Two other ranches along Montana's Rocky Mountain front had sold for over 90 million recently, but he felt he had a greater number of lakes, streams and wildlife on his acreage in addition to superior infrastructure. So certain was Jack of the property's value, he had already planned exactly how he would use the proceeds. After closing costs, he would put 20 million in trust for his grandkids. Another 20 million would go to his children. And last, but certainly not least, his wife would find 20 million deposited into her private trust account. The remainder Jack expected would be needed for taxes and for a new home in town, but with luck, he might have a little left over to splurge on a shiny new jet.

With his assessments completed, Jack made a call to his old friend and real estate ranch broker, Roy Peterson. He knew Roy could sell the ranch for 110 million or more, as the man had both decades of experience and the resources of his large brokerage firm at his disposal.

When Roy arrived, Jack had every bit of documentation on the ranch's amenities and improvements laid out on the big dining room table. Paperwork, blueprints, photos and maps blanketed the entire surface. Jack even had current building inspection reports and proof that every deficiency had been corrected. Roy couldn't help but be impressed by Jack's attention to detail, though his client's plans for the proceeds felt a bit premature.

"So, Jack," Roy ventured, "you think the ranch will sell for 110 million?"

"That's right and maybe more. It's a real bargain."

"It sounds high, but let me take some of these documents with me. I'll spend tomorrow checking on recent sales and the market outlook."

Jack agreed to the plan and they made an appointment to meet up in two days.

On the chosen date, Roy returned with his completed analysis. He also brought along a mutual friend, Elmer Fitzwater - an auctioneer who specialized in the sale of high-end ranches.

"I thought it would be good to get Elmer's input since he's covering six states out West now," Roy explained.

"Glad to see you Elmer," said Jack, shaking the newcomer's hand. "Any friend of Roy's is a friend of mine."

Roy quickly got down to business. "Here's what we have come up with. We think your ranch should be listed at 90 million, which we consider to be at the top of our price range. We believe that range to be 75 to 90 million, based on our evaluation."

Jack interrupted, "But your number is at least 30 million short of what it should be!"

At this point, Elmer chimed in. "Jack, the market isn't backing your number. I've personally looked at or been part of twenty ranch sales comparable to your ranch, and the 110 million number just isn't possible, in my opinion."

"I don't care," Jack insisted. "I know someone will pay my price, and besides, I have important plans for the proceeds."

Roy jumped back in. "Okay, Jack. Here's what I'll do, provided you agree. I'll list the ranch at 110 million for 60 days, and if it doesn't sell, I'd like you to agree to a new list price of 90 million for 120 days. That's six months. After that, we'll go down to 80 million for another six months and then reassess at the end of the year."

Jack gave it a split-second thought. "That's not a problem. I know The Lazy J will sell for my price or close within 60 days. Let's move ahead."

"Okay, Jack," continued Roy, "but I must warn you, we will be trying to sell your ranch for more than it's worth, in our opinion. In a sense, we are conspiring to try and make this sale happen."

"That's okay with me, Roy." Jack grinned. "It's legal isn't it?"

"Of course. You can ask anything you want, but quite often when a property is overpriced, it can affect the final sold price."

Jack waved away Roy's concerns. "We don't need to worry about that. I know The Lazy J is a showplace. It will be in demand and sell at a premium very quickly."

As Roy and Elmer were leaving, Elmer considered sharing more of his thoughts with Jack. Ultimately, he kept them to himself. He was glad to be in the auction business, where a sale was done in twenty minutes or less, instead of taking months or even years to complete. He wanted to tell Jack, "It's the buyer who's going to determine the price, not you." But Elmer didn't think it was his place since he had been invited to just give an opinion on the market.

Jack was quite happy with the results of the meeting. He had always prided himself on his sales ability, and he had sold Roy and Elmer on what he thought was the ideal price. Although he liked both of them well enough, neither one had experienced his level of financial success. Not even close. Jack had started a small software company many years ago, and today their products were distributed worldwide. He eventually sold the company to a competitor for over a billion dollars, which allowed Jack to retire, buy his ranch and make all the improvements that he wanted.

After successfully negotiating his own corporate sale, Jack felt like he could sell anything. He'd decided that Roy didn't have the experience or expertise on how to "think outside the box" and sell at a premium price without his guidance. Both Roy and Elmer were all caught up in their numbers and comparisons, and Jack knew there shouldn't be any comps for a showcase ranch like The Lazy J.

Thirty days later, Roy and his team were ready to bring The Lazy J to market. Preparing the property for sale had been the easiest step in the process. Normally, the decluttering and staging of unwanted furnishings was a painstaking chore. But Roy had been unable to find a single extraneous element within the main residence or the guesthouses on The Lazy J. All of the furnishings had been curated by top designers, and every piece of furniture seemed to have a place and purpose. Jack and his wife had kept up with the times, replacing floors and fixtures whenever a room began to look outdated.

The property was as "photo ready" as any that Roy had ever worked with, so he'd been able to devote much more time to advertising. His team had built a website featuring a series of gorgeous, professionally-edited videos, and they'd produced multiple page full-color brochures using ground and aerial photography. Print ads had been placed in the leading ranch magazines and national newspapers, plus an internet marketing campaign was well underway.

Worldwide outreach would bring awareness of The Lazy J to every possible ranch buyer.

Jack felt quite happy with the campaign, especially since he had helped Roy put it together. If Jack knew anything, it was how to market a product.

Roy kept pitching his own ideas, however. "Jack, I have one item to add. It's my belief that 80% of the marketing is in the price."

"What are you trying to say, Roy?"

"What I mean is: the *price* is our greatest marketing tool. No amount of advertising will sell a property for more than it's worth. If we were pricing your ranch at Fair Market Value, that would do more to sell The Lazy J than any amount of marketing."

"That may be true, Roy, but you are forgetting the quality of the product. I may have my faults, but I know *quality* and I know *products*. Good quality goes for more money. My ranch is a prime example."

At this point, Roy felt ready to move on. He could hardly wait for the next 60 days to be gone. Roy had assigned two of his agents to be present at the ranch every day for the first two weeks to give tours. He planned to station himself there as well in order to welcome prospective buyers and introduce them to The Lazy J.

Within the first week, many calls and emails came in for appointments – far more than Roy expected. There were eight showings scheduled for the following week and another four the week after. This was an unusual number of showings for a ranch, but The Lazy J had gained some renown over the years and had always been listed among the "Top 10 Ranches in America" by Ranch Magazine, Inc.

Jack was beside himself over the amount of interest his ranch was receiving, and he worried that he might have set the price too low. He gave Roy a call. "Should we raise it?"

His broker's answer was a flat no. "Let's see what happens with these appointments first."

A few hours later, Jack got the idea that he could be the Tour Director for all the prospective buyers visiting the ranch. Nobody knew The Lazy J better than himself. Plus, he could sell anything to anyone.

Roy didn't take to this plan, either. "You may be good at selling, Jack, but you have never sold a ranch before." He suggested that Jack and his wife move into their condo in the nearby town for a couple of weeks. Jack reluctantly agreed, on the one condition that he be kept up-to-date on all the showings.

The first tours went well, and the buyers went away impressed. They thought The Lazy J was one of the best ranches they had ever seen... they just weren't sure about the price. Most of the visitors were looking at other ranches, and they said they would come back for another showing if they decided to make an offer.

The next week's tours also went well, but several buyers fixated on the maintenance costs for the golf course. One of the buyers didn't play golf, so the ranch failed to interest him. Another didn't have any airplanes, so the runway and hangar were unnecessary.

Roy reported this feedback to Jack, but the owner responded, "Don't they know the golf course was designed and built by one of the top golf designers in the world? That other buyer could use the hangar for a car collection and the runway could be used as a drag racing track. You need to think outside the box, Roy."

The broker sighed. "Jack, the designers and builders are all listed on the brochures and websites, and we do remind them in person. I've mentioned that the hangar could provide good storage for cars and boats, but I'll admit I didn't think about using the runway as a drag strip."

Roy ended the conversation feeling dissatisfied as usual. The hardest part of this particular sale was having to suppress his gut instincts and career experience. But the listing was relatively fresh. There was still a chance he could be pleasantly surprised.

4

The sixty-day mark came in a hurry. There had been twelve showings, but not a single one resulted in an offer. Roy informed his client that in accordance with their agreement, he was lowering the list price to 90 million. Jack prided himself on being a man of his word, and his family would simply have to do with less money than expected. However, he knew that if he had been at any one of the showings, The Lazy J would have been sold by now.

In the days that followed, two offers came in. The first one was for 88 million. Jack countered at full price but never heard back from the buyer. Roy cautioned that the first offer is often the best one, but Jack responded, "I've heard all that, but I don't believe it. We're just getting started. There will be more offers."

The next buyer wanted the ranch for 85 million, but Jack proved nearly impossible to budge. He finally agreed to a counter of 89 million. Once again, there was no response. Jack couldn't understand why potential buyers failed to recognize the value of his ranch. He told Roy,

"Those two other ranches easily sold in the 90's, and neither of them compares to what I've got here."

"Jack," said the broker patiently, "you're forgetting that one of the ranches had oil and the other was a very profitable cattle and horse ranch."

"Mine has all the potential for that and more."

"But Jack, you don't have it *now.*"

"Okay, but I've got the golf course and the landing field."

"Maybe so, but your maintenance costs are over 2 million per year and are starting to approach 3 million."

Jack remained undeterred. "I know there's someone out there."

They had a couple of additional showings at The Lazy J, but no offers. Jack began to think that using Roy as his broker had been a mistake. Sure, the man had dozens of ranch sales under his belt, but Roy *was* getting older. Elmer was getting up there in years too, and the two of them could just be stuck in their old ways of thinking.

Jack picked up the phone again. "Roy, I have a new idea. What about the Chinese market? They're buying everything. And the Middle Easterners, they like horses."

"We've already covered all those markets, Jack. A few inquiries, but no requests for showings." Roy tried to summarize the feedback he'd received from prospective buyers. The bottom line was that The Lazy J was priced too high and there were too many features that were unusable or unwanted. Some of the potential buyers appreciated the oversized horse stables, the racetrack, the golf course, the landing field or the hangar building. But nobody was interested in having all of those amenities, or even most of them.

Another two months went by, punctuated by a series of

similarly unproductive phone calls between Jack and his broker. Soon, it would be time for another price reduction, and that deadline was enough to motivate Jack to take matters into his own hands. It wasn't the first time he'd had to insert himself into a business transaction. Even within his own company, despite having good salespeople working for him, Jack had occasionally needed to take control in order to get a sale past the finish line.

His first step was to make a list of friends, associates and clients who had visited the ranch over the last decade and had asked to be contacted if the place ever came up for sale. Jack wondered why he hadn't thought of this before. Maybe he didn't even need Roy, except to handle the paperwork. After wracking his brain for an hour, he came up with fifteen prospective buyers. At the top of the list were two Russians who had been his distributors for Eastern Europe. They had gone on to purchase some Russian companies and had become quite wealthy in the process.

Jack chose Abel Baranov as his first target. Abel's assistant Tamara picked up the phone. The woman recognized Jack and said she would transfer him over, though there would be a four-minute delay. It seemed an unusually-precise number, but Jack agreed.

After exactly four minutes, the call went through. "Hello, Jack!" the Russian roared. "Eeet is good to hear from you."

Jack could hear glasses clinking in the background, accompanied by fast-paced music. "I can't hear you very well, Abel."

"Jack, I am on my yacht in the Mediterranean. I will go down to my office." After another minute, the thickly-accented voice returned. "Does thees sound better now?"

"A lot better," Jack replied.

"How is life with you, Jack?"

"Everything's fine. I'm in the process of selling my ranch and you always liked it, so I thought you might have an interest."

"Well, yees, I might have, but now I am into yachting. Thees is where all the action is, Jack. Beautiful women, beautiful weather and everything life has to offer. How much are you asking for the place?"

"I was asking 110 million, but now I'm down to 90 million. A real buy."

"90 million, *huh,*" the Russian snorted. "I paid more than that for this new yacht! Eeet is longer than one of your American football fields. You know, Jack, I just remembered I saw an article about your ranch een one of the Greek real estate magazines. Eeet was quite well done."

Jack realized that his broker's marketing reach was better than he had ever imagined. "Well," he tried, "how about our mutual friend Boris Alexeev? Do you think he'd be interested in the ranch?"

"He might have, but he is no more."

A touch of shock went through Jack's system before he remembered who he was talking to. Even though Abel's English was good, the man sometimes had an abrupt way of expressing himself. "What do you mean, *Boris is no more?*"

"He went out for a walk last summer een the evening and he never came back. I hear lots of rumors and speculation flying around. No one is telling the real story. I was een Monte Carlo last week and his yacht was auctioned off. Eeet was about half the size of mine."

Jack could picture the grin on his old friend's face.

"Too bad," said Jack, "but thanks for your time."

"No problem! After you sell your ranch, you come over here for some of the action."

Jack agreed, though at the moment, the only action he wanted was for his ranch to be sold.

Next on his list was Ralph Emerson - the man who had bought his software company. Jack should have thought of Ralph earlier; not only had the businessman liked his ranch, but many of Jack's old employees were still employed with Ralph, and he was sure they would enjoy visiting the ranch again.

"Hello, Ralph. It's Jack. How's everything going down there?"

"Fantastic," said the CEO. "Sales and earnings are at record levels."

Jack felt a twinge of jealousy. He brushed aside the emotion and said, "I always knew my company and yours would be a good combination. The reason I'm calling is, I have my ranch for sale, and I thought you might have an interest."

"Well, maybe I would have, but my son Ralph Jr. is the new CEO, and he announced recently that we are now "minimalists"."

"What's a minimalist?" asked Jack.

"As I understand it, it means *less is better.* The boy wants everything streamlined. He even talked me into selling the hunting lodge last year. Sorry to say, we won't be a prospect for your ranch, but I wish you the best for success."

"Thanks, Ralph."

Jack wasn't discouraged. He still had twelve people on his list, and one of them would jump at the chance to own The Lazy J. Roy would see.

The next morning, Roy got a call requesting a showing from the office of the famous entrepreneur Billy Andrews. Billy was world-renown as a pioneer in developing apps and turning them into billion-dollar businesses. Besides his corporate success, Billy was also considered to be one of the top amateur golfers in the world. His skills were formidable enough that at the age of 23 he might have joined the pro touring circuit, had he not just made his first billion dollars and become too busy with his companies to go on tour. Now at age 36, his net worth was reported to be 25 billion, and he had gained additional fame for his purchases of trophy real estate properties around the world.

When Roy called to share the details, Jack could barely keep himself from jumping up and down with excitement. "I knew the perfect buyer was out there! Roy, we need to raise the price for this showing."

Roy declined, explaining that the buyer already had the price. Jack agreed to let his broker make the arrange-ments, though he insisted that he be present for the showing. "Billy and I have a lot in common," Jack asserted. "We've both been in a similar line of business, we're worth a lot of money and I've heard he's great at sales, just like me."

Roy thought for a minute as to how he would answer without having to give a flat refusal again. "Jack, you might have some things in common, but there's a lot that you don't. Billy is fifty years younger than you. He's worth 25 times your net worth and he's one of the top golfers in the world. Besides, he is coming to see The Lazy J, not you. If he wants to meet you, that's up to him."

"Okay," Jack relented, "but I'll stick close by for when I'm needed."

On a crisp Saturday October morning, a large, private black jet took a low pass over the Lazy J runway. Roy observed from outside the hangar. The plane executed a climbing turn to the left before coming back around. *They probably wanted to check out the runway before landing*, Roy thought to himself. He looked at his watch and noticed the visitors were ten minutes early but would be right on time once they reached the hangar. As the jet taxied up, Roy felt a current of awe run through him; he had never seen a black private jet before, or any kind of black airplane, for that matter. He didn't know the manufacturer, but it looked fast, even on the ground.

Through the windshield, he noticed that both pilots were women. *Women are getting into everything*, he thought. *They will be selling ranches next.* Then he remembered that his granddaughter had recently asked him about becoming a ranch agent. Things were always changing faster than he expected. *Oh well... whoever can do the job*, he mused.

A man and a woman got off the plane wearing pinstriped business suits and carrying matching leather brief-cases. Roy assumed that Billy Andrews had brought his wife along, but the woman approached him swiftly and held out her hand. "You must be Roy. I'm Carol, and this is Jim. We'll be assisting Billy today. He is still on the plane and will be joining us shortly."

Roy wondered, *whatever happened to the days of people referring to their last names and using Mr. or Mrs.?* He had no idea what he should call these two, and now he didn't know whether to call their employer "Mr. Andrews" or "Billy". He decided he wouldn't assume anything for this particular showing.

Soon enough, Billy stepped off the plane dressed in blue jeans, a white t-shirt and flip-flops, holding his cell-phone and looking like he hadn't shaven in three days. Despite his promise to himself, Roy found his assumptions exposed yet again; he'd guessed that if Billy hadn't shown up in a suit, the man would at least be wearing ranch or golf clothes. Today's showing was bound to be a revela-tion... to what degree, Roy was still unsure.

"Hello Roy, I'm Billy. I recognize you from the website."

"Good to meet you, Billy, and welcome to The Lazy J. Let's go to the conference room in the hangar."

As they entered the building, Roy followed Jack's instructions to point out the size of the hanger as well as Jack's jet and helicopter. Billy's jet was about twice the size of Jack's, but Roy emphasized that the hangar had plenty of room for a larger plane.

Inside the conference room, Jack's assistant had prepared a complete buffet with both breakfast and lunch options. Roy's maps and reports lay spread across the conference table. Billy's assistants sat down and immediately pulled laptops from their briefcases. They informed Roy that they'd already received copies of his reports and had generated several of their own.

Roy tried to appear unfazed. "Great. We'll use the originals for reference if we need them."

Carol got down to business. "All right, Roy. Give us a short summary of the Lazy J's history, improvements and anything else this ranch has to offer."

Roy proceeded to give a rundown of the ranch's past owners, which included a former vice president of the United States and a CEO of one of the largest auto companies in America. He ended his synopsis with a short excerpt of the information Jack had provided about himself. Jack had written three pages; Roy kept it to three sentences. The broker then listed the numerous improvements, including the 20,000 square-foot ranch house, the four other residences, the clubhouse, the hangar, and the golf course, stables and new roads. He pointed out that it took five years and several million dollars to get the runway approved, and the work on these improvements had been undertaken by the most prestigious architects, designers, and builders in the world.

Billy thanked him for the summary. "Before we begin the tour, Roy, I'd like to mention that I've been working on a new real estate app for evaluating ranches in the western states with more than 50,000 acres, including those in Texas and Hawaii. I don't expect this app to net me another billion dollars, but I've always been interested in why real estate sells for less than the list price, or for sometimes a lot less. We're planning to test market the software next year and I believe it can predict what a buyer will pay for a ranch within a range of 5% accuracy. Should the app prove to be successful, we might expand it to cover all types of real estate, including residential. Who knows... it might someday become another billion-dollar app since I haven't seen any real estate web sites that are very accurate." He turned to his assistant. "Carol, please show Roy some of the tools we're using to build the app."

"Of course." She turned her laptop around so the others could see the screen. "On this chart we have plotted the ranches that have sold in the past ten years, those that are pending, and the ones that are currently for sale, plus the acreage. The line you see is the trend line, which is the average distance between the properties and what we call the Fair Market Value Line. It's probably the same input you use, Roy. This chart is just one method of showing market value, as we have developed a weighted point system that accounts for each ranch's improvements and unique characteristics. We can add points for each item, or deduct points if certain features are lacking or not needed. As you can see, this chart makes the market value more vivid for both the seller and the buyer. We call it a Scattergram."

To which Roy replied, "A Scattergram? Sounds like a game I used to play." *Good thing Jack isn't here,* he thought. *Jack would call it a scatterbrain idea.* "Where's The Lazy J go on this chart?" he asked.

Carol answered, "It's right in the middle, within a range of 75 to 90 million."

That sounds rather familiar, Roy thought to himself.

"When the ranch was listed at 110 million," she continued, "it appeared in the upper right corner, almost off the chart completely, meaning it was overpriced." She spun her laptop back around and closed the display.

Billy indicated he was ready to start the tour. "I want to see the golf course and make a short trip around the property so we can make our final calculations. Carol will come with me and report back to Jim on my observations."

Just as they stood up to leave, Roy's cellphone rang. It was Jack. He turned it off. Whatever Jack had to say, it could wait.

☙ 7 ❧

When they were climbing into the van, Roy's phone rang a second time. He considered that it might be it an emergency, so he excused himself and took the call.

"Hello, Jack."

"It's me, Roy. Does he want to meet with me?"

"No, Jack, he's here to see the ranch and we're just getting started. I'll call you later."

"That was some flyover he made, huh, Roy?"

Roy lowered the phone for a moment so his client wouldn't hear his sigh of exasperation. "Where are you, Jack?"

"I'm over the hill by the lake where I can't be seen."

"Jack, go back to town to your condo. We are dealing with a very astute buyer who knows ranches and knows what they are worth."

"That's good, Roy. He'll see how The Lazy J really stands out."

"Talk to you later, Jack."

The broker returned to the van and drove Billy and

Carol to the clubhouse, where they switched to a six-person golf cart. Roy started to head towards the first tee, but Billy forestalled him, saying, "Let's start at the 18th green and work our way back to the first tee. When I look at golf courses for purchase or play, I find that examining the course in reverse gives a much better perspective."

Billy knew the course designer personally and was quite familiar with his work. As they traversed the fairways, Billy made frequent calls to Jim back at the conference room about the course. Roy had never seen a golf course evaluated in such detail, and he turned to Carol to ask what calculations her boss was making.

"He's checking the playability of the course to ensure it won't be too difficult for his guests. Also, he's checking the greens, the bunkers, the fairways and the rough to evaluate the maintenance costs. High costs would affect the value of the course and the ranch. We currently own and operate seventeen courses at our resorts around the world, most with 36 or 54 holes."

Roy admitted that he might be in over his head with this buyer. It would be difficult for Jack to defend his price.

They finished the course and got back into the van to continue the tour. Billy wanted to see as much land as he could in one hour, then visit the main structures. Roy commented, "We won't be able to drive too far in an hour. I suggest we take the owner's helicopter since his pilot is standing by."

"Not necessary," said Billy. "All I need is an hour from the ground to compare to our aerials."

Roy was surprised. "You have aerials?"

The man nodded. "Yes, we photographed the entire ranch two weeks ago from the satellite we just launched.

It gave us the chance to test a new camera system that we developed with our German partners. The images appear to be the best available in today's market."

At this point, Roy was asking himself, *what hasn't this 36-year-old done?* He felt relief that Jack hadn't invited himself onto the tour. His client had accomplished a lot during his life, but that was nothing compared to this young entrepreneur.

Their next stop was the sprawling ranch house, which included every possible amenity a home could have. "It will take some time to see all the rooms," Roy cautioned.

"We can make it quick," Billy replied. "I looked over the floorplans while we were on the plane."

This buyer is ahead of us on everything, Roy thought.

As they entered the house, Roy mentioned that all the furnishings were included and had been custom-made at the time the house was built.

"That makes the furniture 10 years old," Billy observed. "Some might consider them to be *used* furniture."

Roy had to keep a tone of defensiveness from creeping into his voice. "Well, it's top quality," he said, and let it drop. Billy and Carol didn't seem to hear him; they had already started their own tour, drifting from room to room.

Ten minutes later, they reappeared. "We can head to the guesthouses now," Roy suggested.

"No need for that," Billy replied. "I just want to see the stables."

"Sure, Billy. What did you think of the ranch house, then?"

Billy finished sending off a text on his phone before

answering. "I think with a few changes it might work for my employees and customers."

"What about for yourself?"

The young man scratched his chin, considering. "I'm not sure if I would be staying here overnight, but if I did, the master would need major changes."

Is this guy for real, Roy thought, *or is he just trying to justify a lower price?* He couldn't wrap his head around the idea that anyone would spend millions on a ranch and not intend to ever sleep there. He had to remind himself that this was not a normal buyer.

After a quick trip to the stables, they began to make their way back towards the hangar and the conference room. Billy spent much of the drive on his cell phone, sharing more of his observations with Jim. During a free moment, Roy suggested it would be a good idea to review the tour and answer any of Billy's remaining questions.

In hindsight, the broker could have predicted the response. "No need for a review, Roy. We have everything we need, and it's time for us to be on our way. It looks like we may be making an offer on the ranch, subject to the new data we've collected. You have seen the Scattergram, and you can expect that our bid will be what we perceive as market value, which is likely what any other buyer would do. Thank you for your hospitality, and please express our thanks to the owner."

"You are welcome to take any food from the conference room with you," Roy offered.

Billy shook his head. "No thanks. We'll be having an early dinner on the plane before we land in New York."

Roy sensed an awkward silence was coming. There was nothing more to be said, so he shook hands with the businessman and left it at that.

※ 8 ※

Roy stood within the shade of the hangar, watching Billy's plane as it roared down the runway, climbed into the Montana skies and disappeared. He had never had a showing like this one, and he probably never would again. Just then, his cell-phone rang.

"Roy, did you see that takeoff? All that power!" Jack's voice had a teenager's jealousy layered over a toddler's giddy enthusiasm.

"Where are you now, Jack?"

"I'm at the far end of the runway, hidden, but where I could get a good view. It looks like we've found the right buyer. He plays golf, has a plane, and likes horses."

"That's all true Jack, but if he makes an offer, it will be based on what his staff has calculated as market value. Plus, he doesn't plan to spend much time here."

"You mean he's not going to be here full-time?"

"He told me he would rarely spend the night. One of his assistants said that he owns seven other homes around the world."

"That must be nice," Jack groused. "By the way, I don't want to hear any more about *market value*. It doesn't apply to The Lazy J. My ranch has its own market, which is way above any so-called *market values.*"

"Okay, Jack. Let's just see what happens."

"What's the next step, Roy? Should I write him a personal note and thank him for coming here? I could tell him how much I've enjoyed the ranch and all its special qualities. I know how to write notes and put some real pizazz into them."

"No, Jack. We wait to hear from him and hope it's an offer."

❧ 9 ❧

The next morning, Roy's phone rang. This time, it was his old friend and ranch broker competitor, Wilbur Strange.

"How's it going, Roy?"

"Not bad, Wilbur. We just had a good showing of The Lazy J yesterday."

"That's what I heard. I wanted to let you know that I'll be representing Billy Andrews, and I'm working on an offer."

Roy was caught off guard. He thought this transaction would be his and his alone.

"How do you know Billy?"

"I've known him for some time," Wilbur explained nonchalantly. "I've been helping him purchase properties around the country."

Interesting. "He didn't mention anything about you yesterday."

"He wouldn't have. He likes to look at places on his own, then bring me in if he decides to make an offer."

Roy let out a sigh, then asked, "When can we expect the offer?"

"It should come within an hour, by email."

Roy gave Jack a call to tell him the latest. "We're expecting an offer within the hour, Jack. It's coming from Wilbur Strange, who's representing Billy."

"Wilbur Strange?" Jack blurted. "How did that character get involved?"

"He said he'd helped Billy purchase other properties."

"Fine. I'm sure he'll offer top dollar. The Lazy J fits him perfectly. Let me know the minute it comes in."

"Will do, Jack."

Within forty minutes, Roy's computer lit up. The email from Wilbur came through with an attachment. Roy opened it quickly and saw that the offer was for 75 million, all cash with a 10-day close and no inspections. The property would be purchased as-is. It was a very clean offer, but Roy knew that Jack would balk at the price.

Reluctantly, he dialed his client. "Jack, I have the offer. It's all cash, no inspections, and it will close in ten days."

"Roy, you left out the *price.*"

"He wants it for 75 million."

"What?" Jack sputtered. "Are you sure? Someone worth 25 billion can pay my price. The Lazy J has everything he needs! This is a big disappointment, Roy. A *big* disappointment."

Roy tried to keep his voice even. "Jack, I've never known you to pay more for something than you thought it was worth."

"Well, I'm a seller, not a buyer. And besides, my ranch is exceptional!" Even over the phone, Roy could tell that Jack's blood pressure was rising. "Did you tell Wilbur what a big discount I'm already giving off the correct price of $110 million?" Jack continued. "Or that someone will easily come along and buy it out from under that pompous billionaire?"

"No, I didn't. But Billy knows the market and is apparently offering what it's worth to him. He also doesn't care anything about other buyers."

"This offer is so low, I want to counter at full price. If he doesn't accept it, well, we can contact the buyer that offered 88 million and let him have the ranch."

"Jack, that gentleman bought another property, and the 85 million buyer decided he no longer wants a ranch." He tapped his fingers against his desktop. "Look, I'll talk to Wilbur and find out if there's any flexibility in Billy's thoughts about the price."

That got him off the phone with Jack, at any rate. He punched in Wilbur's number. "Hey, it's Roy. We got your offer. Seems low, right?"

"It's what Billy thinks the ranch is worth," Wilbur explained, "and I agree after looking over his computer model. He's come up with quite an app... I don't know if you've seen it. One of the ranch's problems is its high operating costs and lack of adequate income."

"All right, Wilbur. Jack wants to counter at full price, but I'm going to recommend something lower."

"I would be careful with counters," the broker warned. "When Billy makes an offer, he believes his offer to be Fair Market Price or very close to it. He won't do more than one or two counters. The man will walk away before he does any more."

"Okay, Wilbur. I'll see what I can do."

Roy didn't waste any time getting back to Jack. "I talked to Wilbur. The problem, as they see it, is the high maintenance costs, which effects what Billy is willing to offer."

"That's ridiculous!" Jack protested. "A man worth 25 billion can easily spend 2 to 3 million a year on upkeep."

Roy had another thought. "Let me talk to Elmer and see what he thinks about the offer."

"Fine."

Roy was fortunate; the auctioneer picked up the phone after a few rings. "Elmer," he began, "Jack has an offer of 75 million for The Lazy J. What do you think?"

"I'd say that's a good offer. The J is a beautiful ranch with many amenities, as you know, but it needs a buyer who can afford it as a hobby because of the high operating costs. If I were going to hold an auction for The Lazy J, it would probably bring around 80 million, based on my other auction sales."

"Thanks, Elmer," said Roy sincerely. "I'll let you know what happens."

"Sounds good," the auctioneer replied. "Seems like this buyer knows the market."

Roy got Jack back on the line. "All right, Jack. Elmer thinks 80 million would be the Fair Market Value for The Lazy J."

"I can't believe this! I would have a loss of at least 30 million if I sell at this so-called *Fair Market Value.*"

Roy felt his patience evaporating. "Excuse me, Jack, but can you explain that to me? I thought you would have a gain, since you paid 25 million and invested 30 million in improvements for a total of 55 million. That should work out as a gain of 25 million."

"Oh no, Roy. Your calculations are incorrect. I would have a loss of at least 30 million since my price was 110 million."

At this point, Roy wondered, *how did this man ever make a billion dollars?* "Jack," he tried, "since we are good friends, I can tell you that 110 million was a "Dream Price"."

"Okay, maybe you're right," Jack admitted. "I may have been thinking too far into the future, but since you're asking me to accept a lower price, we need to talk about your commission."

Roy didn't like the sound of that. "What do you mean, Jack?"

"Well, to make it fair, you need to share in the lower price by lowering your commission."

The broker paused for a moment before speaking. "I'm already taking a lower commission since the sales price will be lower. Besides, half the commission will be going to Wilbur now, and I've incurred considerable expenses in marketing your ranch. Is there a reason you would want to penalize Wilbur and me for bringing you an all-cash, 10-day close and contingent-free offer after six months on the market and no other offers in sight?"

"Okay, okay, enough already," Jack relented. "I know what I agreed to do regardless of the sales price. It's just hard for me to sell so low and take such a big loss." He took a moment to collect himself. "What do we do next?"

"We need to counter Billy's offer," Roy began, "but two counters has to be our limit. Wilbur said that's all Billy will consider, and he'll walk if we try to drag it out beyond that. He's looking at other ranches."

"What price do you recommend for our counter?"

"I would recommend 80 million. That's 5 million more than he offered. I think if we tried 85 million he might counter, but then again, he might not. Elmer agrees that 80 would be a good price, but it's your property and the decision is yours."

Roy swore he could hear Jack grinding his teeth on the other side of the phone. "Okay, I'll do it," Jack finally said. "I'll just have to find more money somewhere else."

Roy found himself asking, "Jack, why do you need to find more money? You have plenty. You don't owe anything on the ranch... in fact, you don't owe anything, period, as far as I know."

Jack took no offense. "I know, it's just the idea that I won't be getting my 110 million price for this exceptional property. That miser is getting quite a deal. Make sure he has the money. I want to see account statements. Some of these new big shots are *all hat and no cattle,* as they say in Texas."

R oy got the counter prepared and sent it over to Wilbur. It came back in less than an hour, accepted and signed for 80 million. He quickly called Jack to give him the good news.

"Congratulations, Jack! Our counter was accepted. We'll be closing in ten days."

"Yeah? Does he have the money?"

"We'll find out. He has to show proof of funds in 24 hours and make a $2,500,000 deposit at the same time."

Roy was soon on the phone again with Wilbur, explaining that Jack insisted on seeing account statements, not just some letter from a bank.

"Not a problem, Roy," Wilbur reassured him. "The funds were just wired to escrow."

"That will take care of the deposit, but-"

Wilbur interrupted, "Roy, you don't understand. Billy doesn't show anything to anybody. Look, the entire 80 million has been wired to escrow. Do you think that will work as proof of funds?"

Once again, Roy found himself in awe about the nature

of this transaction. Even after fifty years in the business, he had never seen the full price sent with a final counter or with *any* offer. Still, he resolved to appear as cool and collected as possible. "Yes, that will do, Wilbur. I just received confirmation from escrow. Thank you for all your work."

"Thanks for your part too, Roy. Now let's get it closed."

Roy gave Jack a call to report on the latest developments. Everything was moving fast, and Jack had a hard time keeping up.

"Are you sure it's real money, Roy? I guess it's a good thing we cleared out our personal items when the ranch was listed. I was sure it would sell within 60 days back then. Well, I'll need to get my plane and helicopter moved over to the town airport."

"Yes, it's real money," Roy confirmed, "and you will be the owner for only ten more days, Jack."

Jack let out a long breath. "You know Roy, I've been thinking. Maybe 80 million isn't such a bad price. If I kept the ranch another ten years it would have cost 30 million in maintenance and operating expenses. It's like I'm actually getting my price of 110 million. You know what I mean, Roy? 80 million plus 30 million equals 110 million."

Roy wasn't sure about Jack's logic, but if the numbers finally worked for him, so much the better for everyone.

The Lazy J closed right on schedule. Billy excused himself from the proceedings, but six of his staff flew in and moved straight away into the ranch house. They informed Roy that they'd be evaluating the renovations that needed to be done and conducting interviews with the current ranch staff.

Jack had moved the last of his possessions into his condo. It made for crowded living conditions, but the retiree expected to buy another house before too long.

As for Roy, the broker was busy planning a much-needed vacation when his phone rang.

"Hello, Roy. It's Jack. Thanks again for getting The Lazy J sold. I've spotted a house at the country club that I want to buy."

Roy had to ask, "Is it for sale?"

"No, but when the owners find out that I'm interested, they will want to sell. I know how to buy."

"Of course you do, Jack." Roy leaned back in his chair. "I'm on my way out of town, but my granddaughter can help you make an offer. She's been with me for only two months, but she has a mentor working with her."

"Sounds great. I like working with young people and I can teach her how to buy and sell real estate, no problem."

Roy was grateful his client couldn't see the wry smile on his face. "Sure, Jack. I know she will appreciate your advice and knowledge. Good luck."

EPILOGUE

R oy had a lot of time to think about The Lazy J while on vacation. He thought Jack's ranch was a textbook example of what happens when a property is overpriced. As soon as he got back, he started planning a presentation for the next real estate company meeting, and he invited Elmer Fitzwater to participate because of his auction experience.

They held the meeting two weeks later, while Roy's thoughts on the Lazy J listing were still fresh. After his agents shuffled into the conference room, Roy took out his notes and launched into the topic.

"Good morning, everyone," he began. "The first item on our agenda is the recent sale of The Lazy J Ranch. Several of you were involved in this sale along with Elmer Fitzwater, who I invited to be with us today. The Lazy J was a classic example of what you can expect to happen if you overprice a property. Elmer went with me to the listing appointment. I had done a complete analysis and came up with a listing price range of 75-90 million. In addition, Elmer looked back at his auctions and he concurred with my estimates. Do I have that right, Elmer?"

"That's right," said the auctioneer. "Looked at a lot of other similar auctions, too."

"Unfortunately," Roy continued, "the owner believed his ranch to be worth 110 million and he insisted that this should be the listing price. I finally relented, so long as he would agree to lower the price to 90 million if it didn't sell in 60 days. He accepted my proposal fairly quickly because he was confident the ranch would sell during the initial time period."

"We had a great turnout at first, with twelve showings scheduled over three weeks and many additional inquiries. This might be considered unusual for a ranch this size, but The Lazy J was well known and it always listed among the "Top 10 Ranches in America" by Ranch Magazine. We received no offers during the first 60 days, however. After lowering the price to 90 million, we had two offers, one at 88 million and another at 85 million. The seller countered at full price and we received no response from either buyer. As the six-month mark approached, I had an unexpected call from a new buyer. He made an initial offer of 75 million, and we settled on a final price of 80 million."

He scanned the faces of the agents in the room to make sure they were paying attention. "The question on a transaction like this is always, *what would have happened if the Lazy J's first list price was 90 million, not 110 million?* Anyone want to give an answer?"

Homer Jenkins raised his hand. Homer was one of Roy's older agents with forty years of experience. "It seems to me that with the number of showings you had with qualified buyers, there would have been multiple offers if the price had been 90 million."

"Thank you, Homer. Elmer, how do you think the property would have gone if we'd auctioned it instead?"

"I think half of those buyers at the showings would have been bidders if the list price had been 90 million. I would have started the auction at 75 million and the bidding could have gone over 90 million and closed within thirty days. Also, I'd point out that there would have been more potential buyers at the showings if the starting price was lower."

Orville Jennings, another experienced realtor with a thirty-year sales record, spoke up. "What I've found through the years is that if you price a property at Fair Market Value or close to it, a buyer will recognize it as a good buy. They will perceive the property to be good value and they'll put it on their preferred list. I've personally found this to be true for all price ranges."

"Thanks, Orville," said Roy. "Anyone else?"

Julia Peterson, Roy's granddaughter, raised her hand.

"Yes, Julia?"

"I'm the new one here, but it seems to me that it's not just the right price that is important, but the *timing* of the right price. You have to get it right in the initial listing, or at least soon afterward."

"Good observation, Julia. Thank you." He turned back to the group. "Well, one thing we know for sure is that we had an offer of 88 million and ended up at 80 million. The lesson learned is that if you as agents do your homework, the list price is going to be very close to the final sales price. Whenever the process gets drawn out because of an overpriced listing, the seller ends up losing money and we end up with a lower commission."

"What we *can* do – and this is the reason I called you all in today – is keep telling stories like this one, and do a better job educating the seller. With this transaction in particular, a good example of client education was the buyer's use of a Scattergram, which put The Lazy J in perspective for both himself and the seller. The buyer came up with about the same value that Elmer and I had reached, but the graph made the correlations much more vivid and convincing. We also learned from the buyer's agent that he had no intention of seeing the ranch or making an offer when the list price stood at 110 million. That's another example which shows why buyers don't make offers on overpriced properties."

Roy collected his notes into a pile and tapped them for emphasis. "As a final thought, I would add that most sellers are not like the one I worked with at The Lazy J. They have a more realistic expectation as to what their property is worth. But we still need to provide an accurate price range and make sure the listing reflects Fair Market Value right at the outset."

As his agents trickled out of the conference room, one of the younger agents, Tom Bradford, came up to Roy.

"Thank you for the presentation, Mr. Peterson. It was very educational. You should write a book."

"Oh, you think so, Tom?" Roy smiled. "What would it be called?"

"Price Right and Sell High."

ACKNOWLEDGMENTS

Many thanks to those that took the time to read the original manuscripts and offer encouragement and suggestions, including Birgitta Baker, Michael Cohen, Jan Finley, Cindy Jones, Joyce Enright, Jo Ann Mermis, Willard Thompson, Frank McGinity, John St. Clair, Ken St. Clair and Tanya Wheway. A special note of gratitude to my editor, Bryan Snyder, who always has a way of deriving sense and order out of my words and phrases.